This Book Was Donated
To The Tenacre Library By

name: Martha Anne Lauer

date: 7-26-91

CHINESE MOTHER GOOSE RHYMES

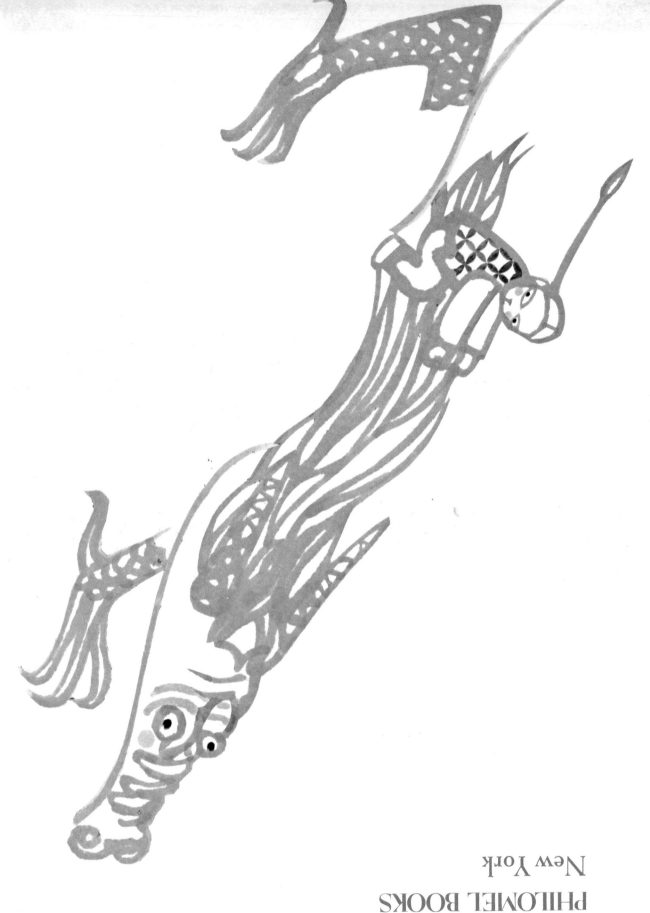

PHILOMEL BOOKS
New York

CHINESE
MOTHER
GOOSE
RHYMES

Selected and Edited by
Robert Wyndham
Pictures by Ed Young

For my brother Jim,
the best of big brothers.

Published by Philomel Books, a division of the
Putnam & Grosset Group. Published simultaneously in Canada.
Original hardcover edition published 1968 by The World Publishing Company.
Illustrations Copyright © 1968 by Ed Young. Special contents of this edition
Copyright © 1968 by Robert Wyndham. All rights reserved. Sandcastle Books
and the Sandcastle logo are trademarks belonging to The Putnam & Grosset Group.
Printed in the United States of America.
First Sandcastle Books Edition, 1989
Library of Congress Cataloging-in-Publication Data
Main entry under title: Chinese Mother Goose Rhymes = (Ju tzu ko t'u)
Parallel title in Chinese characters.
Summary: A collection of nursery rhymes translated from Chinese,
including ones on lady bugs, kites and bumps on the head. Also includes
the rhymes in Chinese characters.
1. Nursery rhymes, Chinese. (1. Nursery rhymes)
I. Wyndham, Robert, date. II. Young, Ed, ill. III. Title: Ju tzu ko t'u
PZ8.3.C443 1982 398.8 81-21030   AACR2
ISBN 0-399-21718-5 (Sandcastle pbk)
First Sandcastle Books Impression
First Philomel Hardcover Impression

LIST OF FIRST LINES

The poems in this book are all traditional. Some have been translated especially for this collection. Others have been selected from one or the other of these two books:

Pekinese Rhymes, collected and edited with notes and translations by Baron Guido Vitale, published in 1896 by the Pei-T'and Press, Peking.

Chinese Mother Goose Rhymes, translated by Isaac Taylor Headland, published in 1900 by the Fleming H. Revell Company, Westwood, New Jersey.

AUTHOR'S NOTE

Every country has its nursery rhymes and ballads for children, and in the different languages they vary in style or detail. Yet children's poetry the world over is also amazingly alike in other respects and it is correct to speak of it as being universal.

There are the similar lullabies. There are the counting songs with three as the common denominator. Other counting rhymes which are for fun as well as instruction involve the fingers or toes. Universally, there are poems about animals, flowers, good and bad children, people who are tall, short, thin, or fat. So the reader of this book should find himself comfortably at home with the presentation in English of these Chinese nursery rhymes.

Of course no amount of scholarly knowledge can reproduce in English an exact equivalent of Chinese poetry because of the vast differences in the structures of the two languages. However, the basic human emotions, subjects, themes, and plots can be reasonably approximated in the writing transference. My versions in English are meant to convey the spirit, the feeling, and intent of the originals, yet render them freely enough to interest and entertain English-speaking readers and listeners. I hope this book will bring pleasure to every one of them.

—ROBERT WYNDHAM

Morristown, New Jersey, 1968

太陽出來一點紅
師傅騎馬我騎龍

師傅騎馬沿街走
我騎蚊龍水上游

As the sun came up, a ball of red,
I followed my friend wherever he led.
He thought his fast horse would leave me
    behind,
But I rode a dragon as swift as the wind!

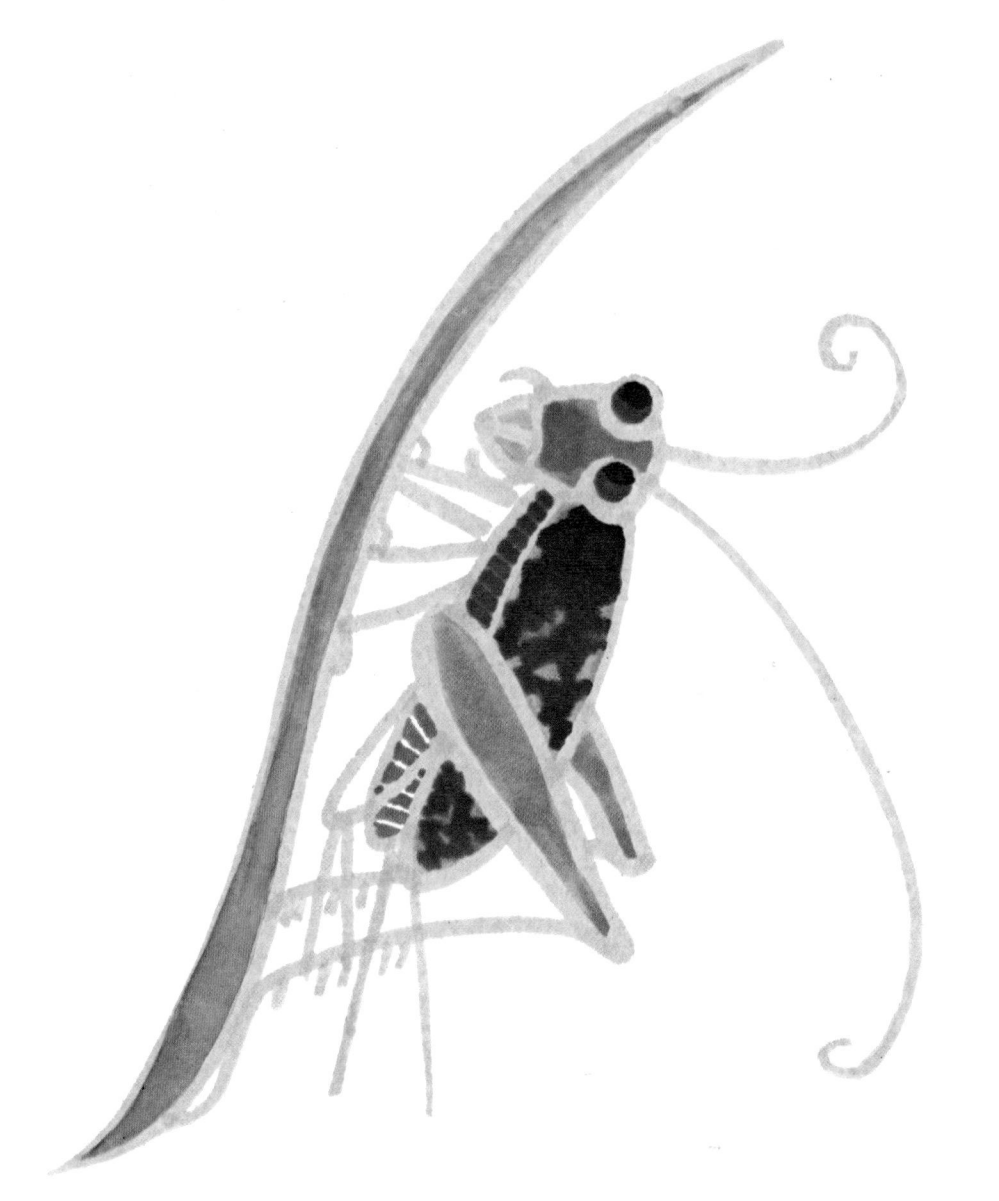

高高山上一顆蘇有個吉了兒往上爬

我問吉了兒你上那他說渴了要吃蘇

On the top of a mountain
A grass blade was growing,
And up it a cricket was busily climbing.
I said to him, "Cricket,
Now where are you going?"
He answered me loudly, "I'm going out dining!"

蟲蟲蟲蟲飛到南山吃露水

Lady bug, lady bug,
Fly away, do!
Fly to the mountain
To feed upon dew.

Feed upon dew
And when you are through,
Lady bug, lady bug,
Fly home again, do!

露水吃飽了回頭就跑了

蝴蝶落我不要

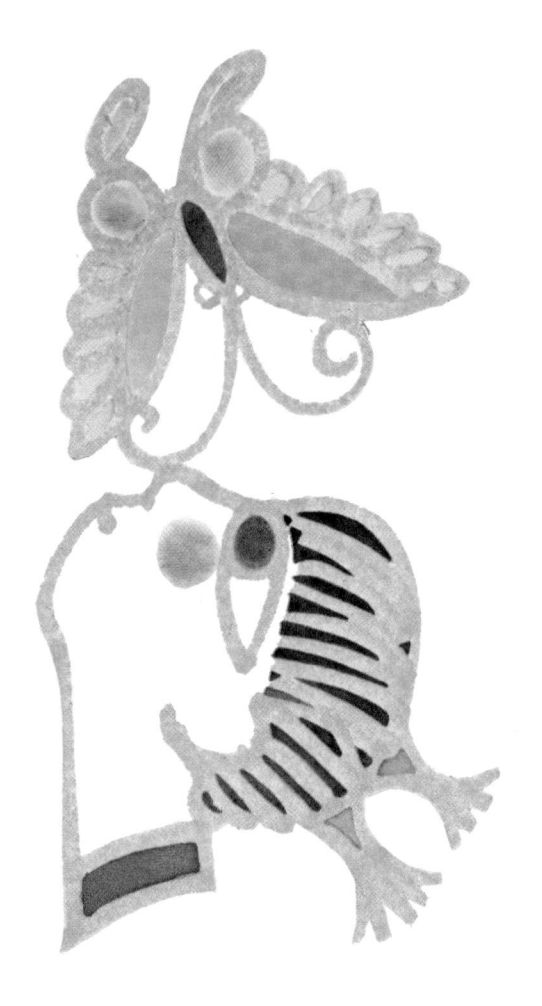

蝴蝶飛我不追

Away floats the butterfly.
To keep it I would never try.

The butterfly's about to 'light;
I would not catch it if I might.

小眼兒看景致兒小鼻子聞香氣兒

Little eyes see pretty things;
Little nose smells something good;
Little ears hear someone sing;
Little mouth tastes luscious food.

小耳朵聽好音兒小嘴巴吃玫瑰兒

小棹子兒 小椅子兒 烏木筷子兒 小碟子兒

小小手兒 開鋪兒 開開鋪兒 兩扇門兒

A wee little boy has opened a store
For serving up food, at his front door.
There's a wee little table, a wee little chair,
Some ebony chopsticks, and a wee bowl to
　　share.

Flowers for sale!
Flowers for sale!
Come, buy my flowers
Before they grow stale!

不買花花就壞

買花來買花來你

This little fellow
A naughty trick did play
So they sent him to the melon patch,
Far, far away!

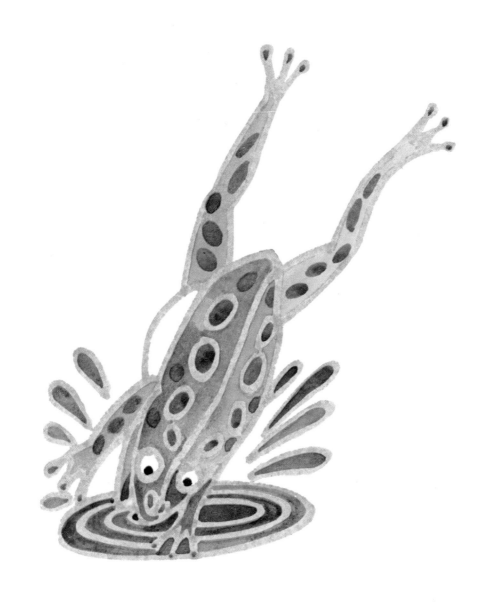

河蟆河蟆跳搭搭東洋大海有他家

閒來無事叫嘎嘎不叫爸爸叫媽媽

Froggie, froggie.
Hoppity-hop!
When you get to the sea
You do not stop.

Plop!

He climbed up the candlestick,
The little mousie brown.
And he climbed up the candle—
But he couldn't get down.
He called for his grandma
But his grandma was downtown,
So he curled himself into a ball
And rolled himself right down.

前剪子兩把
又快子四雙

Old Mr. Chang, I've heard it said,
You wear a basket on your head;
You've two pairs of scissors to cut your meat,
And two pairs of chopsticks with which
    you eat.

What is it?

Turn the page to find out.

老張老張頭頂破筐

The answer

(a crab)

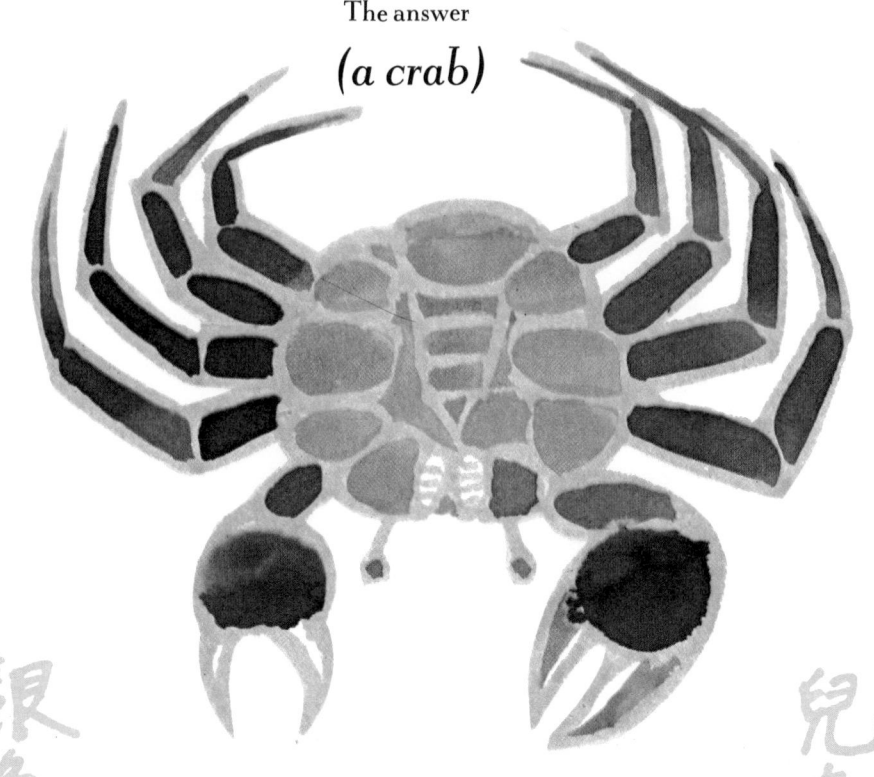

If you chance to be crossing
The camel-back bridge,
Each step leads you higher
Till you come to the ridge.

The lantern grass floats
On the pond like a sail,
The silver fish bites
At the gold fish's tail.

The fat green frog,
Sitting there on a rock,
Croaks out his greeting,
"Warrah! Warrock!"

蝦蟆石上坐着哇兒瓜哇兒瓜的叫

銀魚兒咬着金魚兒尾大肚子

兒高燈兒龍兒闌草水皮兒深

羅鍋子橋羅鍋子橋一磴到比一磴

一隻船兩頭高渾身沒板淨生毛

天天要裝紅糧米船底無縫可漏腳

My boat is turned up at both ends;
All storms it meets it weathers.
On its body you'll find not a single board,
For it's covered all over with feathers.

Daily we fill it with rice;
It's admired by all whom we meet.
You will find not a crack in my boat,
But you'll find underneath it two feet!

What is it?

Turn the page to find out.

The answer
(a duck)

Little snail, little snail,
With your hard, stony bed,
First stick out your horns
And then stick out your head.

Your father and mother
Have brought some roast meat;
So come, little snail,
Please hurry and eat.

But where has that little snail gone,
Please do tell?
He's turned right around and
Gone back in his shell!

水牛兒水牛兒先出捔角後

出頭兒你爹你媽給你帶來

的燒羊肉你不吃不給你留

在那兒呢在墳頭兒後頭呢

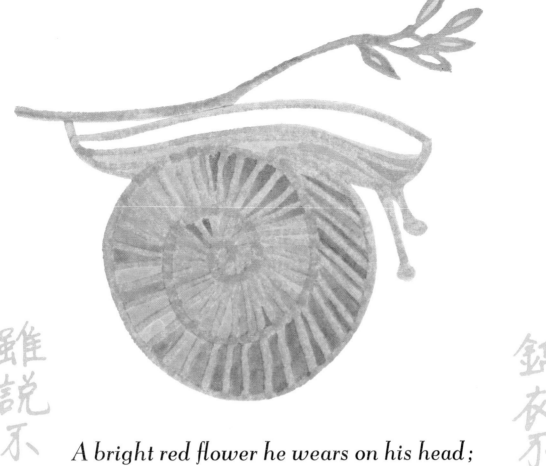

一朵芙蓉頂上栽
錦衣不用剪刀裁
雖說不是英雄漢
一聲喊叫萬門開

A bright red flower he wears on his head;
His beautiful coat needs no thimble nor
    thread;
And though he's not fearsome, I'll have you
    know
Ten thousand doors open when he says so!

What is it?

Turn the page to find out.

麵粽子臉
梅花腳
坐着倒比
站着高

What has feet like plum blossoms,
And a pudding-face sweet,
And is taller when sitting
Than when standing on its feet?

What is it?

Turn the page to find out.

(a rooster)

(a Pekingese dog)

同來瞧同來瞧，耗子長了一身毛

同來看同來看，黑雞下了個白雞蛋

Come and see!
Come and see!
A black hen has laid
A white egg for me!

要袴要掛天河吊角要袴要袄

天河打斜吃瓜吃茄天河劈分山

When the Milky Way you spy
Slanting stars across the sky,

The eggplant you may safely eat,
And all your friends to melons treat.

When it's divided toward the west
You'll need your trousers and your vest.

When like a horn you see it float
You'll need warm trousers and a coat!

It has eyes and a nose
But has not breathed since birth;
It cannot go to heaven
And will not stay on earth.

What is it?

Turn the page to find out.

上不了天下不了地

有鼻有眼不喘氣

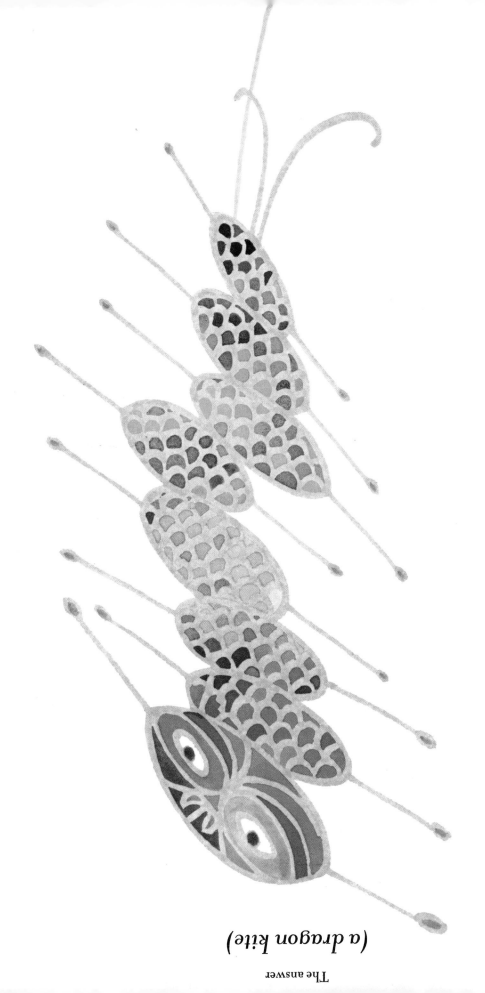

大姐放的花蝴蝶活娛蚣飄飄起在空好似一條龍

Two little sisters went walking one day,
Partly for exercise, partly for play.
They took with them kites which they wanted
    to fly,
One a big centipede, one a great butterfly.
Then up in a moment the kites floated high,
Like dragons that seemed to be touching
    the sky!

姐妹二人到城東一到城東去逛青捎帶放風箏

你媽穿着乍板鞋走一步蹋拉拉十箇指頭露着三

小禿兒咧咧南邊打水是你爹你爹戴着紅纓帽

Dear little baby,
Don't you cry;
Your father's bringing water
From the brook near by.

A red-tasseled hat
He wears on his head.
Your mother's in the kitchen
Baking you some bread.

See, from mother's shoe tips
Peep three pretty toes!
Now baby's laughing,
There he goes!

楊樹葉兒嘩拉拉小孩兒睡覺找他媽

乖乖寶貝兒你睡罷媽虎子來了我打他

Willow leaves murmur, hua-la-la.
Sleep, precious baby, close to mama.
Hua-la-la, baby, smile in your sleep;
You'll have only sweet dreams
While my watch I keep.

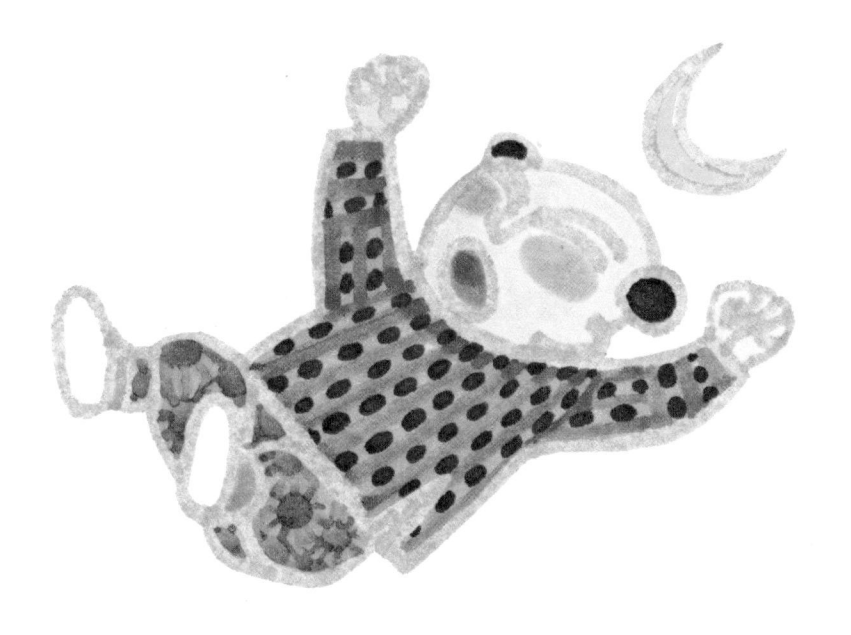

天皇皇地皇皇我家有個夜哭郎

過門君子念三遍一家睡到大天亮

The heaven is bright,
The earth is bright,
I have a baby who cries all night.

We keep a dog to guard the house;
A pig will make a feast or two;
We keep a cat to catch a mouse;
But what is the use of a girl like you?

養活豬吃口肉養活狗會看家養活

貓會擎耗子養活你這丫頭作甚麼

爬草根兩頭分路中來了小學生騎花馬拜丈人丈人丈母不在家推

開門來看見他粉紅臉賽桃花小小腳兒一柄把櫻桃小口糯米銀牙

As the sun rose over the mountain,
A student came riding along.
He sat on a dapple-gray pony,
And sang a scrap of a song.

To the home of his bride he was going,
And he hoped that she wouldn't be out;
He saw as he pushed the door open
The girl he was thinking about.

Her cheeks were as pink as a rosebud.
Her teeth were as white as a pearl.
Her lips were as red as a cherry.
Most truly a beautiful girl!

Beat the drum! Rum-pum-pum!
Here comes someone in a carriage chair!
Rum-pum-pay! Clear the way!
It's a bride who's riding to her wedding there.

Rum-pum-pum! Beat the drum!
The carriage chair is drawing near.
Beat the drums! Here it comes!
Now the way is clear.

新年來到糖瓜祭灶姑娘要花子要炮老

頭子要買新氈帽老婆子要吃大花糕

You'll find whenever the New Year comes
The Kitchen God will want some plums.
The girls will want some flowers new;
The boys will want firecrackers, too.
A new felt cap will please papa,
And a sugar cake for dear mama.

疣瘟疣瘟下去別叫奶奶看見

奶奶若看見不給我們飯錢

Bump, bump, please go away.
Don't let mother see you.
If she finds you there on her baby's head
She'll give me no money to buy my bread.

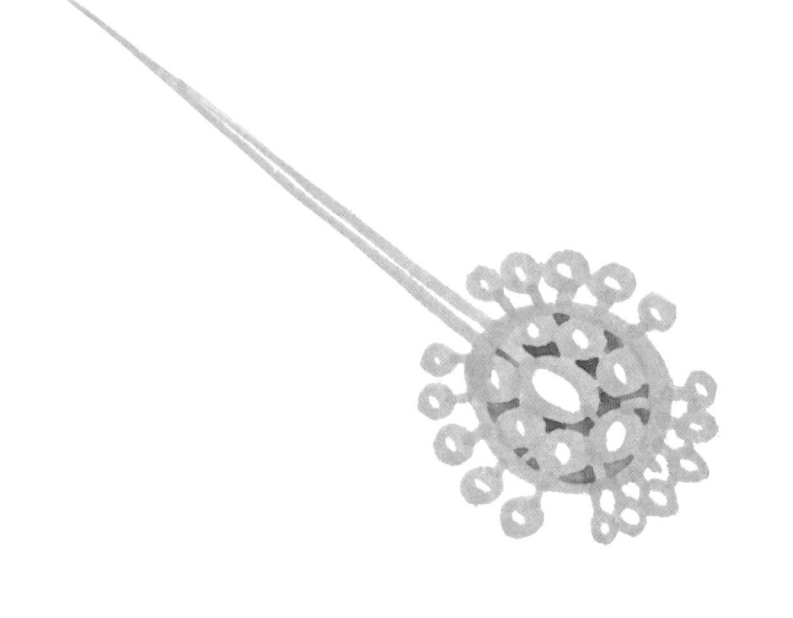

On the top of the hill,
By the road, on a stone,
On a big pile of rocks
Sat a bald-headed crone.

On her head were three hairs,
Which you see were quite thin,
In which she was trying
To fasten a pin.

She put it in once
And at once it fell out;
She put it in twice
And twice it fell out.

But the old woman said,
"I know what I'm about;
I'll not put it in—
Then it cannot fall out!"

高高山上一羅圈上頭坐着土奶奶三根頭髮挽個髻兒一

心要戴兩操鬆基一戴一出溜二戴又出溜不戴不出溜

這個人生來性兒急清晨早起去

打集錯穿了綠布褲倒騎了一頭驢

A hurrying man he always was,
From the day that he was born;
And to hurry to a fair one day
He rose at early morn,
Put on his wife's green trousers
To hurry to the sale,
Jumped on his little donkey
With his face toward its tail!

高高山上有一家十間房子九間塌老頭子出來拄拐棍兒老

婆子出來就地兒擦看家的狗兒三條腿避鼠的貓短尾巴

On a very high mountain
A family dwell;
They once had ten rooms
But nine of them fell.

The poor old man walks
With a great deal of trouble;
His wife hobbles after,
Her body bent double.

Their three-legged dog
Is as thin as a rail,
And their rat-fearing cat
Is minus a tail.

忽聽門外人咬狗拿起門來開開手拾起狗來打磚

Outside my door, I heard someone say,
A man bit a dog in a vicious way!
Such news I ne'er for a moment could stand,
So I lifted my door to open my hand;
I snatched up the dog with a slow double-quick
And tossed him with force at a very soft brick.
The brick—I'm afraid you will not understand—
I found in a moment had bitten my hand.
So I mounted a chair, on a horse I was borne,
While I blew on a drum and beat on a horn!

頭又被磚頭咬了手騎着轎子擡了馬吹了鼓打喇叭

My little golden sister
Rides a golden horse so slow;
She'll have to use a golden whip
To make her slow horse go.

A little golden fish
In a golden bowl has she;
And a golden bird is singing
On a golden cherry tree.

A smiling golden Buddha
In a golden temple stands,
With a tiny golden baby
In his gentle golden hands.

小金坦騎金馬金馬金鞭打琉璃井金蝦蟆梧桐

樹金老鸛開了廟門金菩薩金手帶鸛金娃娃

高高山上一個牛
尾巴長在屁股後

四個蹄子分八辮
腦代袋長在脖子上

There's a cow on the mountain,
The old saying goes;
At the end of her legs
Are four feet and eight toes.
Her tail hangs behind
At the end of her back,
And her head sticks out front
At the end of her neck.

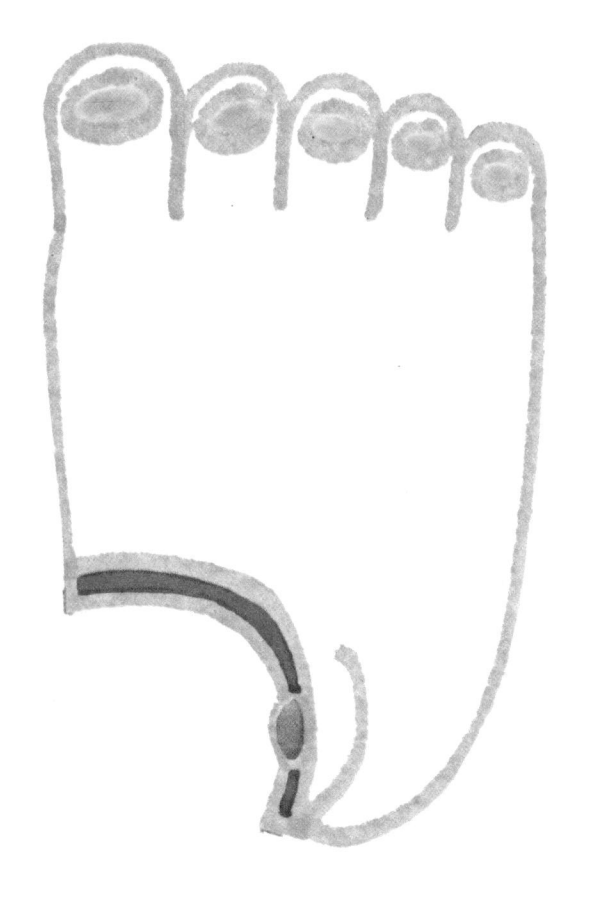

這個小牛兒吃草這個小牛兒吃料這個小牛兒喝水兒

This little cow eats grass,
This little cow eats hay,
This little cow drinks water,
This little cow runs away,
And this little cow does nothing
But lie down all the day.

這個小牛兒打滾兒這個小牛兒竟臥着我們打他

老和尚背鼓來咯

The wolf has come,
The tiger has come,
The old priest follows,
Beating a drum.

狼來咯虎來咯

拉大鋸扯大鋸用木頭

盖房子給貝貝娶娘子

We push, we pull
To saw up the wood.
(We pull, we push)
We make a fine house.
(We push, we pull)
It has to be good
(We pull, we push)
To keep a sweet spouse.

(A Rocking Game)

So you be a roller
And roll with power,
And I'll be a millstone
And grind the flour.

(A Twirling Game)

了油撒了你是碾子我是磨

大狗上京了小狗跑了雞蛋砸

餅激溜軲轆一個

Gee lee, gu lu, turn the cake,
Add some oil, the better to bake.

Gee lee, gu lu, now it's done;
Give a piece to everyone.

(A Turning Game)

翻餅烙餅油查餡

你追我我追你

喊得喊喀得喀

A peacock feather
On a plum-tree limb,
You catch me
      and
         I'll
           catch
             him!

(Blind Man's Buff)

上去下來羅蔔要買水壺要拿偕們瞧咯天上瞧什麼月亮星星地

裏瞧什麼水井井裏瞧什麼蝦蟆蝦蟆說什麼起來格尔瓜格尔瓜

Up you go,
　　　　Down you see,
Here's a turnip for you and me.
Here's a pitcher, we'll go to town.
Oh, what a pity! We've fallen down!
What do you see in the heavens bright?
I see the moon and the stars at night.
What do you see on the earth, so near?
I see a frog, and his voice I hear.
What is he saying there on the rock?
"Get up, get up! Warrah! Warrock!"

(A Lifting Game)

398.8
CH

Chinese Mother Goose
rhymes

$14.95

DATE			
10/4/91 K			
8-1-93 Hernandez			
OK			